PREP WORK

P.D. SINGER

ROCKY RIDGE BOOKS

Prep Work © P.D. Singer 2014

Breaking the Fast © P.D. Singer 2014

Cover art by Cosmic Designs

ISBN-13 978-1-62622-045-4

First printing Dreamspinner Press 2011

Second printing Rocky Ridge Books 2014

Published by:

Rocky Ridge Books

PO Box 6922

Broomfield, CO 80021

http://RockyRidgeBooks.com

PREP WORK

I was desperate to eat something without an audience. Nobody but I would know what the sip from the glass was, no one else was entitled to an opinion of the contents of my plate, no one was there to tell me, "Have another bite. Do it again."

No camera tracked every morsel from plate to palate tonight; I could not take another request for a do-over of some tidbit that only the crazy or the starving—or the locals—would willingly put in their mouths. Maybe Renfield wanted another taste of the morsels I was expected to eat until Sam the Sadist and Marcie the Monster were satisfied that the light values and the grotesquerie of my meal were properly captured on film, but I did not. I wanted good, honest lager, poured with just the right amount of foam on the head, and a snack of something that the English-speaking world recognized as bread with a bit of cheese that didn't smell like dead men's feet. I wanted to chase it with a pickle that looked like it began life in a garden, not the bottom end of a cave in ancient Gondwanaland. And damn it, no one was going to take pictures of it going into my mouth. I would chew in privacy for what might be the first time in weeks.

I know, that sounded ungracious, especially since I had the best job in the world—going from continent to continent eating my way through the best cuisine in the neighborhood, telling the camera and therefore the folks down home how delicious it all was. Or how stomach turning. Or how the gnocchi and risotto in Parma, Italy stacked up to the same dishes served at Mama Rosa's in Parma, Ohio. I've been from Phoenix, Arizona way past Tahoma, to Bombay, to the back-ass of beyond in Thailand and Kenya, munching my way through whatever the locals offered me. Sometimes I thought they were having way too much fun at my expense. Sometimes they'd fight me for what was on the plate. Sometimes I felt like an unmitigated ass for taking even a mouthful away from people who work too fucking hard to collect enough food for family groups who are way too kind about taking in the ugly American who can't even say "thank you" properly in their language. I always worry about it coming out as the local variant of "fuck your mother." I'm not much of a linguist.

I didn't have to practice words I didn't understand here. We might be divided by a common tongue, but any insult I offered to someone's mother would be on purpose, because we were all speaking English, more or less. Me, probably less. At least by local—UK —standards.

But that's okay; I wasn't saying a word here. I was drinking a pint of lager—that's "beer" to my fellow Yanks and "one type of beer" to people who are accustomed to a lot more choices—that's sitting at the perfect temperature, not too warm, not too cool. Best of all, I'm not explaining to anyone or their camera about the best way to cellar the stuff, something I'd become an expert on about seven minutes before the camera rolled.

The traveling circus that is *Jude Marshall Tastes* had been left behind for the moment, and I had no doubt that Sadist and Monster were using the room to its fullest capacity before we flew back to the US. I would come back later and try not to breathe deeply of their escapades. It was just for one night; we couldn't connect flights from Nowhereskavi to New York without the layover. Sharing a hotel room kept the expenses down, which was entirely necessary both because it was the end of this filming tour and because—have you ever priced a hotel room in London? The producers should thank us for watching the money. Oh, you thought I was the tall guy with the earring and the big budget?

I wish.

No, I'm the "me too" guy, with a smaller channel, a smaller budget, and a bigger need for the outrageous just to get noticed. You might say I'm the guy most likely to have to eat spider on a stick.

Wasn't supposed to be like that. I had a great restaurant with a following and a Michelin star, a cookbook to compete with barefoot royalty, sexually frustrated olive oils, and quick meals plus adorable accents. Then it all faded away, except for the lawsuits. Let's just say that my financial backer and I don't exchange Christmas cards any more, although he does remind me of that non-compete agreement every time he hears I've pitched a project. Bastard.

I was a sort-of somebody, and now I'm a different sort-of somebody, lucky to have a gig that at least takes me all over the world and into new experiences. It keeps me afloat in a sea of chefs and ex-chefs all looking for their own personal formula for "Bam."

A month of eating my way through year-old cabbage and roast pig parts in Bumfuckistan and adjacent locales left me yearning for something immediately recognizable. Comfort food. So when the waitress came along to ask if I wanted anything else, I stopped her after the words "pea soup" left her mouth. I liked the irony of eating pea soup in London, I wanted a flavor that reminded me of home, and I wanted honest, unadorned thick green glop that sat in the spoon until bodily removed. Pea soup never sounded better.

Pea soup went with the ancient carpet in this pub and the tables carved with graffiti. Perhaps I would go shoot a few darts after I ate and give Sadist and Monster another few minutes alone with a mattress that sagged like the Marianas Trench. It wasn't like I had anyone who wanted to crawl into any sort of bed with me. Life on tour was hard on a relationship, something that made the producers' first-choice chef back out before the contracts got printed. They found me after that, alone, unattached, not even a cat to feed or an aquarium for someone else to clean. Being a chef in a fixed location is hard enough on a relationship, with the crazy hours and the various temptations, whether it's the bottle or the food or the waiter in section three.

I do have qualifications for this gig beyond being unattached and willing to eat food not found in American supermarkets, though I draw the line very firmly at *balut*. I can describe what I'm eating, and my tendency to say any damned thing I think was at last a power harnessed for good, though at forty-two, I should fucking well be able to speak my mind. Lacking a filter south of brain, north of mouth got me fired from more than one job in my youth and had figured into losing the restaurant, but was probably a bigger asset now than my "piercing amber eyes," my "ruffle-able brunet hair," or "semi-athletic physique" or any of the other bullshit the publicists had written into the promo material. The audience hardly ever saw my eyes anyway. They were usually closed, either from the joy of a heavenly grilled prawn or the horror of quite a lot of things. And they're light brown, damn it.

Don't get me wrong. I'm glad that my crew found each other. They were away from their settled lives just as much I was, if you could call what I had back in New York "settled." With just the three of us, any tensions between them were likely to slop on the third party, and that sounded a lot like "Have another spider on a stick, Jude."

I'd had enough of the tensions and food I could barely pronounce—this tour was over just in time, and I could leave Sadist and Monster behind for a few hours while I started to soak back into my own life. A beer and pub grub were a good place to start.

I didn't want weird, I didn't want fancy, I just wanted—

And the waitress was back now, with a bowl that contained thick green soup and—

"Oh fuck. What is this?" I picked up a few shreds of the frizzly stuff on top and let it flutter back to the surface.

"Parsley." She gaped at me like I was an escapee from Broadmoor or wherever they stashed the lunatics these days.

I held my head, shaking it back and forth, muttering, "Oh fuck, oh fuck, what is this, I can't, no, no." Or words to that effect. It was parsley. But why did it float on top of my soup in this corner pub, where I expected simple, solid fare?

"I'll take it away then." She reached nervously for the bowl, but I stopped her.

"It's not your fault." At least I hoped not; wait staff in my establishments never garnished the food. "Don't mind me. It's been a rough couple of weeks." She snatched her hand back. Couldn't blame her.

"It does say on the menu…." Her gaze darted to some authority lurking behind her.

How did I miss the big green chalkboard marked with the day's specials? Though why would a pub even need one? Sure enough, colored chalk lettering described fresh green pea soup with chiffonade of prosciutto and parsley and noisettes of something in something sauce that I couldn't read from here. The words of doom were in bright yellow and should have sent me running before I got my jacket off. Gastro-pub.

I've been drinking in a gastro-pub. No wonder the wait-ress goggled at me when I'd asked for a ploughman's lunch.

I picked up the spoon. "It'll be fine." And it was fine, it was better than fine, it was damned good soup —the parsley and the prosciutto added a bit of salt and savor with the nip of chlorophyll. The flavors worked beautifully, the better for being out of place and out of my expectations. I'd always thought good beer and fancy food didn't happen in the same places. Beer and basic went together and never ventured near a white tablecloth. I'd shoveled about a third of the bowl inside when something else out of my expecta-tions happened. Too bad the camera and crew were back at the hotel, because the man in chef's whites was very photogenic: early thirties maybe, thick, light brown hair and creamy skin, straight nose. Where'd he come from?

"Is something wrong with the soup?" he asked, and now I had to explain. I'd upset his staff, and possibly him, with my little tantrum.

"It's spectacular soup. There's something wrong with me." Only one corner of my mouth smiled. "I've been eating a lot of strange things lately, and was all set for something plain. I just wasn't expecting this. I think I walked in with my eyes shut." Shrugging and taking another spoonful of his concoction by way of apology, I met his eyes, only to drown in the depths of blue and concern.

"I suppose you have. Where have you been filming?"

I told him, and didn't think to be startled by the

question until I recited the geography. "How do you know?" I wondered out loud. "Do you watch?"

"Sometimes. Bit of a mixed experience in Thailand for you, poor bloke." His smile brought out a dimple in his right cheek. "I didn't think I'd ever have Jude Marshall sitting at one of my tables. Have you hidden the camera crew?" He glanced around, as if a grown man holding a Sony SRW-9000 on a Glidecam might be crouching under the lip of the bar.

"I'd make arrangements with you first. Really, I'm just here for a quiet meal." Was he disappointed at not getting the publicity? Did he think we'd just barge in? I'm an uncouth SOB, but I have some manners. And if I didn't, I'd still have Managing Marcie.

"Then sorry to interrupt." That smile wasn't an interruption. "But since this might never happen again, I'm going to ask for an autograph. Would you mind?"

Being recognized didn't happen so often that I'd gotten used to it, or that the thrill of being asked had worn off. I patted my pockets, hunting for the stack of business cards I'd left back at the hotel. "Sure. On what?"

His smile was brilliant, full of white but not quite straight teeth. "I've got your cookbook."

I lost my heart completely. He had a copy of my darling! My poor, flash-in-the-pan magnum opus that never came anywhere near the best-seller list, and he had a copy. Hope he didn't understand how rare that made him. "Perfect."

"I've got to get back to the kitchen, but I'll be back out in a minute." Then he did a double-take at the door, where six people had just walked in, filling his face with "uh-oh." "I'll send the book out with Imogen. Thanks."

He nearly ran back to the kitchen: I doubted he'd left something char-able on the burner. If it was all the same to him, I'd rather not wait for Imogen, who would tell me his name but not how to inscribe the book. I would like another look at mine host, who had a very nice ass, even disguised in baggy chef's whites. Finishing off the soup a little faster than it deserved, I threw a handful of change from four different countries on the table for a tip. There were only a few places he could have gone, and when I stuck my head through the likeliest door, he was there, chopping for all he was worth.

"Problem?" In my one burst of discretion for the month, I hesitated to invade another chef's turf and waited to be invited the rest of the way in.

"You could say that." He attacked an eggplant with his big knife. "They're regular customers, always wanting the same thing, whether or not it's on the menu. They've been away for a while, and I wasn't expecting them tonight."

Looked like a one-man operation back there—the pub was small. "I could help."

"Would you mind?" The panic in his face drained away, and I wouldn't bring it back by asking about any public health regulations; I just stepped to the sink to wash my hands. He handed me an apron. "They always order aubergine parmesan."

It had been a while since I'd been in the kitchen, but my knife skills went back twenty years. I hadn't forgotten how to reduce a pile of herbs to fine green flakes, and the onion fell into small squares under my borrowed blade. He had to be scared, or he would never have handed me the knife; I would rather share my toothbrush or my favorite toys than my knives.

"Any advice on making a sixty-minute dish in thirty?" he asked.

He started dredging the slices of eggplant, or aubergine, but whatever you call it, it still takes too long to cook when you start with big purple fruit and the diners are already seated. "Don't tell anyone we committed this crime against food." I tossed his carefully breaded slices into the deep fryer and hoped he'd bought a non-bitter variety.

The eggplant was hissing away and the onions caramelizing in the pan when he finally put out a hand. "Tommy Bell. Thanks for the help. You're a life-saver."

"Glad to do it." Silently we assembled the parm in individual baking dishes. He had the sauce hot already, and it was a matter now of layering and sprinkling, then shoving it all into the oven to brown on top. Imogen was coming through with the orders, exactly as Tommy predicted. The meals would be out in good time, especially since Tommy took the precaution of sending out a little *amuse-bouche* to keep them occupied. "What are you giving them?"

Tommy paused with his serving spoon over a small plate. "White beans and figs in a citrus dressing. It's the side for the chop tonight. They'll eat one bean at a time, say 'oh' and 'ah', and still order the aubergine next time."

"But they keep coming back." I'd had customers like that too.

He was in no hurry to chase me out, and another four-top order came in. Tommy had no *commis* or *sous-chef*, but he did seem to have four or six arms, the way he assembled the food, flinging things from his *mise en place* into small copper pans and making a quick trip into a walk-in fridge, which didn't seem to have any beer in it. Not that I checked. He sent Imogen to the cellar—*Yes! A real cellar!*—for another beer, which he handed over with a slightly lopsided smile that I was coming to like very much. Every kitchen I'd ever worked had been hot, but this one was volcanic. The heat source plated the food, brandishing a squeeze bottle.

"If the parsley upset you, this is going to make you bawl your eyes out." Tommy shot an expert squiggle of sauce that smelled of adobo and peppers over a breast of chicken.

"Boo-hoo." I enunciated each syllable clearly. "You're waging a single-handed battle against the repu-tation of British food."

"Not so single-handed." He passed plates to Imogen, pausing to wipe a thumbprint off a rim. "Though I might be the only soldier around here."

I hadn't laughed so easily or so genuinely with anyone in a long time. Then he reminded me that I'm a celebrity and he's a fan. Damn.

"I'll get the cookbook. It's upstairs in my flat. Be right back."

Alone in the kitchen. I hadn't been there in a long

time. My restaurant closed three years ago, and I'd worked guest gigs now and then, but not in one of my own. This one was small but could be arranged more efficiently. Two of us working together had been just on the edge of tight, but he'd danced around me with great surety for a man who usually worked alone. He was taking a while. The timer on the parm rang. Didn't know when he'd be back, so I grabbed a dry towel for a hot mitt and extracted the dishes. A sprinkle of the parsley on top—*that* was where it belonged—and six dishes were ready to be whisked out to the surprise table as if Tommy had known in advance they were coming. Imogen gave me a funny look but no lip. Then she handed me a ticket.

Tommy hadn't returned. Maybe he'd stashed the cookbook at the very back of the closet. Or in a box he hadn't unpacked since he moved. Five years ago. I could make up a lot of unpleasant scenarios, but right then I was going to make some kitchen magic, because there were hungry people and no chef.

Little pork medallions sizzled in a copper pan and parboiled pasta was ready to dip back into the hot water bath when Tommy returned, holding the hardback medium quarto volume that was my modest contribution to culinary reading. He hugged the book to his chest, his free hand trying to cover three edges at once and his eyes downcast, but I didn't know why—that book was used. Well-used. Little wrinkled spots on the dust cover announced where it had gotten wet, sauce marks decorated the edges of the pages, and dog-ears on the corners peeked through his fingers. Oh. Maybe he'd got it second-hand and never opened it.

"Sorry to make you wait, Jude. I shouldn't have answered the phone." Tommy took an appraising look at the ticket, then at my pans. He smiled and added a spoonful of capers. "You didn't have to cook."

I shook the pan, flipping the shallots and tomatoes over rather than breaking them up with a spoon. "I'm enjoying myself. It's been a while." His hand flashed back to the corner of the cookbook, migrating it into his armpit. I couldn't possibly sign it if nothing but the spine was visible, and even that was getting covered with his baggy sleeve. "How would you like that inscribed?" I flashed him a smile and slid the pasta into the hot water.

"Um…." He stared at my hands.

"I'll get out of the way." I'd taken over. *Way to go, Jude, this isn't your kitchen.*

"You aren't in the way. I like watching you work." He fumbled the book open to the flyleaf without looking at it. "I learned a lot from your book, and…."

He had? The title is *Scaling Down* and the recipes came in two forms: one, the way the pros would do it in a restaurant with servings for fifteen to thirty, plus a companion recipe for family-sized batches that serve four to six with some simplified techniques and standard American kitchen measurements, not metric. I thought it was a good idea, and so did my publisher and agent. All of us were taken by surprise by the irritation of the book-buyers who thought they were getting a diet plan and didn't appreciate the butter and heavy cream. Maybe he had put the sauce stains on himself.

"I can keep going if you like. Another set of hands might be good here." Imogen came by with a ticket, which she held uncertainly, not sure who to give it to.

"I'll take it." Tommy examined the order. "I put the book upstairs because it was getting too messy. I made photocopies of the recipes I use the most." He started another sauté pan heating, and I plated the pork. "A lot of my customers come to eat your food."

I didn't know what to say. Thank you? Oh, good? Do it right, then? "I'm glad they keep coming back." We skirted each other carefully, me with loaded hands and him holding the book against his chest, protecting it from the steam hissing from the pan.

Imogen bustled away with my efforts, but Tommy wasn't turning loose of the book. I wasn't seeing stiff upper lip, or a stiff anything else, but I didn't know what was going on. "How would you like that inscribed?" I asked again.

Glancing down at his pans, Tommy looked like he was blushing, though it could have just been flushing from the heat of the kitchen.

"Or have you changed your mind?"

"No, I haven't. I—" He peered through his lashes at me with indecision and something else. "If you sign it, then you'll go, and this will be over and I'll never cook another dish with Jude Marshall, and—" Tommy sputtered to a stop. "You must think I'm a right prat."

"A bit of a fanboy, but not a prat." How awful was prathood?

He handed me the book. "You decide. You just came in for a quiet bowl of soup, and here I am wasting your time." The pans needed all his attention. Right.

"No, you aren't, and I don't have to leave. Not if you don't want me to." Sam and Marcie wouldn't miss me, and Tommy would. I scrawled *Try chervil on the pea soup sometime* and my name on the flyleaf.

"I don't, if you don't mind staying." His words were hesitant but his hands were sure, which relieved me; I didn't want to have to treat a burn. He had chef's hands, marked, rough, and with the extra padding nature gives the fool who tries to pick up hot objects too often. Mine had softened with time away from the big gas range.

"So, are some of your soups rowdier than others?" Could I get him to laugh?

"My soups are all very well-behaved. It's the customers you've got to watch. You wouldn't believe some of them, slagging off poor, innocent bowls of soup." The glint was back, and so was the dimple. "Ever had that sort in your place?"

"Awful, just awful," I solemnly agreed, trying not to burst out laughing. "They're hardly worthy to be served." Then we did laugh, and I felt forgiven.

So I stayed. And we cooked. And we chatted. I prowled his shelves and walk-in, looking for clues to his style of cuisine, and it was something I could appreciate: honest, fresh ingredients, treated simply and allowed to shine, mixed with a few more complicated preparations.

"How long have you been open?" I asked.

"The pub's been here seventy years. I took over as landlord four years ago." Tommy sprinkled a pinch of salt over the asparagus he was sautéing. "People are getting used to finding something other than a blob of soft cheese in a baguette here."

I didn't mention that I'd come in looking for exactly that. "What kind of hours do you keep?"

"The old hours. Last orders for drinks at eleven, everyone out by eleven thirty." He picked up on what I'd really asked. "The kitchen closes at nine thirty. Then clean up."

"I'll go play dish pit. Will that speed you?" He had no one else to deal with the growing stack of dirty plates, and after he made one quick dash to the sink and then back to the stove, I could see what needed doing. He had the cooking under control. He didn't have his face under control—his jaw was hanging open. I laughed. "It won't be the first time I've been in soapy water to the elbow."

I scrubbed away, enjoying the simple pleasure of bringing order out of chaos and messing with Tommy's mind at the same time. Maybe he could lose the fanboy thinking if he saw me doing the menial tasks that never end. Once everything was loaded in the sanitizer, I ambled back to the stove. "Have you decided on a special for tomorrow yet?"

He shook his head. "I'll wait and see what's good at the market."

I liked that philosophy. Also, I was eaten with curiosity. No mouth to brain filter, remember. "Of all the books out there, why mine?"

"A couple of reasons," he mumbled, his head practically in the oven where he browned the top of something sticky. "I couldn't afford to go to culinary school, so I bought books and took a few classes when I could. I'm still not much of a pastry chef. But I learned by cooking the family portions and then scaling up."

I'd thought his knife work was a little odd, and his *mise en place* barren, not organized as I would have set it up and missing ingredients he'd needed several times during the evening. "You do well for self-taught."

"Thanks." He waved his hand at the rack of spices and metal pans. "It could be more efficient, but I just don't know how to do it. When I washed dishes at Claridge's, they chased me back to the sink every time I tried to look."

Chopping an onion at the moment of need wasn't at all efficient. That should have been done hours ago and replaced if it was used up. I would have screeched harsh words at any of my staff who'd done that, but I'd thought at the time that he just didn't use it much. "Some of my best line cooks started as dishwashers."

"Lucky them." Tommy slid a filet of cod from pan to plate, dribbling the cooking juices over the fish. "When my dad died, any chance of learning elsewhere went too. I had to run the pub or sell it, and it's been in the family since it was built." The asparagus glowed jewel green next to the brown-drizzled white flesh, beautiful in the fluorescent light for the scant seconds 'til Imogen took it away.

No choice then. My mouth didn't ask my brain—I heard myself offer. "I could show you a few things."

To see his face, you'd think I'd brought the sunshine

for the picnic. "Start by showing me exactly how you minced that onion so quickly."

So I did, and began to get a better feel for how much extra effort Tommy had to go through with each day's cooking for not knowing the basics. "You'll pick up speed with practice. Do the shallots similarly or they look like worms in the dish." Perhaps I didn't really have to touch his hand to show the small circular motion that keeps the blade from slicing through the root end prematurely, but I wanted to, and he didn't shake me off.

He peeled another onion to test his new skill. "I've just been slicing them at random. This is a lot better."

That started me asking about his menu changes and thinking how to reorganize his *mise en place*. Tommy didn't need to keep the truffle oil away from the heat; he hadn't gone that far down the path of *haute cuisine* as to have any, but we shuffled pans and plotted prep work until Imogen interrupted us with a late request for shepherd's pie.

"I do cook some of the pub classics, Jude." Tommy scooped out a portion and offered me a taste.

"Mmm. Made with the freshest shepherds?" Delicious, savory with lamb and rosemary, the potato smooth but with enough texture to show it had never been a dehydrated flake.

"He was fresh, all right. I had to slap the cheeky bastard to get him under the mash." He disappeared into the walk-in with the pan, my chuckles following.

The riposte was my reward, along with his blue eyes dancing below the thatch of straight brown hair that stuck out below his baseball cap. Had he sported headgear as pretentious as a toque, I wouldn't have followed him to the kitchen.

"I'll start cleaning up, Jude. Thanks." Tommy glanced at the clock. "I can squeeze a few more minutes from each hour now."

I started scraping the grill. "It's a start." I hadn't really touched on more than the very basics, but his day had been long already and how the hell had it gotten to be nine thirty?

"You don't have to stay for this. You came in for some food, not to end up cleaning a grease trap." He lifted the cover, making a face at the nastiness inside.

"You get to clean your own grease trap. I call mopping the floor." I was reluctant to leave, both for the company and for the joy of creating something delicious, some small bit of edible art. It had been so long, and clean-up felt like payback for the chance. "I'm staying." The mountain of pans in the sink shrank under my hands.

"You really are a lifesaver." He came to stack the dishes from the sanitizer rack, standing a little closer to me than the space required.

Have to find out sometime. "I'm a small, round candy with a hole in the middle?" Did they have those candies here?

He looked confused, but went with the words, not the sense. "Oh, I'm sure there's a hole on you somewhere." He leaned his shoulder against me.

My rate of washing dropped to zero. "It's even been licked once or twice." I leaned back. "I'm not at all cherry-flavored."

"Wouldn't mind checking that out for myself, if you fancied staying the night. Unless"—his eyes flickered to the cookbook, set aside from the prep surface—"he's still tasting?"

"Him" being my former lover, mentioned in the author bio on the dust jacket. I hadn't thought how much of myself I was exposing in those few lines. "Lives in New York City with his partner, Paul" had gotten me some critical brickbats, but this time I was grateful for the "out and proud" comment. "Not for a couple of years." Not since he'd learned the scope of restaurant temptations. "No one else regular."

"That's the anti-social hours for you. Makes it hard to meet anyone." One last bit of pressure against me, and then he went to drag the wheeled bucket and mop from a closet. "Harder to keep them unless they know what it's like already."

One thing I did not understand yet, and needed to. "I'm saying 'yes' either way, but are you asking Jude Marshall the chef, or are you asking Jude, the man?" How much of myself could I bring to his bed?

He didn't answer that right away, running water into the bucket for a few minutes first, and giving me hope for an honest answer. "I asked the chef to sign my cookbook, and it was probably the chef I asked to stay once I came back to the kitchen." He dipped the mop into the bucket, but yielded it when I reached to fulfill my promise about washing the floor. "And you must have a thousand begging for it. But it's the man I'm asking upstairs. I can't get to know you better if you leave."

Not a thousand like him. Not even one like him. I'd bring all of myself upstairs.

We climbed two flights of stairs to his apartment, which took up the back end of the floor past the door marked 2B. He carefully reshelved the cookbook in the bookcase next to a brown loveseat that might have been in the family as long as the pub had. Tommy led me to the bathroom, which looked as if it had been carved out of the larger space. "Would you like to wash the kitchen out of your hair?" Tommy stripped his sauce-spattered, double-breasted jacket off. He threw it at the hamper, though one stubborn sleeve dangled out.

Now that we were out of danger of Imogen popping in on us, I couldn't wait to get my clothes off and peeled myself more efficiently than any shallot I'd ever touched. The ancient claw-foot tub had a thin, white curtain on a floating ring and a handheld shower sprayer, but before Tommy could turn on the water, I had to give myself a little appetizer. I took him in my arms for the first kiss of the night.

Stiff at first, he relaxed against me, melting like butter too close to the stove, and he was the first to part his lips. Tasting, savoring, we explored, and I wouldn't have known he'd kept his eyes open if I hadn't too. I wanted to see him react to me as well as to feel him. I wanted to examine this man with every sense I possessed. Slipping a hand down his bare back brought me a little moan, and a deep sniff against Tommy's cheek plunged me back into the kitchen. I wouldn't let that scent go until he made me.

"Not yet. You smell too good." I stroked my cheek

against his on the way to his neck; it was late enough that our almost-stubble rasped together, and then I could breathe deeply of warm Tommy and his craft. The butter and herbs that had glazed the filet clung to his hair, faint traces of the spicy tomato-based sauce for the eggplant wafted from his skin, and I tried to devour them all. With tongue and lips I explored him, food scents mixed with his own at his neck gave way to salt and sweat on his shoulder, his forearms again bearing hints of what he'd handled and washed away from his hands. That didn't keep me from sliding his fingers into my mouth.

Somewhere on him, there would be clues to everything he'd touched tonight. I would find out what he'd made before I arrived. I had to lick into the hollow above his clavicle and found my way back to his lips. "You taste so good just like this."

I had tasted like that once, and did again tonight, with the time we'd spent together cooking. Tommy was doing his own best to lave the traces from my skin. His tongue and lips against my neck made me hard, and I couldn't help pushing against his groin, scratching against the baggy pants that I hadn't managed to shove off his hips. Kneading the big muscles of his butt with one hand inside the pants and one out, I wasn't going to get those pants off unless I was willing to let go. I wasn't, not before I was completely drunk on the taste of him.

Tommy solved my dilemma by twisting around, letting me grope and press my erection into his crack while he undid the fasteners, the skin of his back smooth against my chest. The sun never had a chance to brown him. He was pale and salty beneath my tongue, and yes, he was hard and smooth under my hand. I had hold of his cock almost before he had the zipper down, firm and hot, the skin slipping over the glans with my slow strokes.

"Let's at least get to the bed, Jude," Tommy mumbled into my ear. He let his head fall back onto my shoulder and found my earlobe with his teeth. Fortified with kisses, I let go long enough to follow him to the double bed before I dragged us down to the cold tile floor of the bathroom instead.

He lay warm and lithe under me on the cool cotton sheets, meeting me thrust for thrust with hips and tongue, his fair skin pale gold under the light of a small lamp. I did my best to touch every square inch of him, no longer hidden under layers of baggy fabric meant to protect him from the dangers of his trade.

He felt good, too—not thin, not fat, just warm and hard, and as eager to absorb me as I was him. His hands traveled up and down my back, sliding to my ass now and again to pull me more tightly against him. With lips and mouth he explored me thoroughly, licking, nibbling, and using the slightest edge of teeth against my neck. I wound my fingers into his hair, sliding along the slight dampness of the inevitable kitchen sweat. Tommy's mouth would feel just that good on my cock.

I nibbled him first, nuzzling my way across the little prickles of hair on his chest, down to his treasure trail. The scent changed along the way, the spices and oils giving way to the tang of a man who'd done honest work. He'd not just earned his bread, he'd baked it. If he'd fed me liquor, it couldn't have intoxicated me more.

Tommy groaned for me when I sucked him in, swiping my tongue along his shaft on the ups and downs, feeling his foreskin bunch and straighten, teasing the edge of the head. No words now, nothing more than *good, oh good,* buzzed through my mind, and then it got better when Tommy urged me around and over him to take my cock in his mouth.

Wet, firm pressure, the slight yielding of lips and the flicking undid me. The little spangles behind my tightly closed eyelids were a pale reflection of the fireworks below. I convulsed and shot my pleasure into a sudden chill. Forgetting to breathe, I fell forward, taking him deeper, and that was enough; Tommy came before I stopped pulsing, and I swallowed almost without tasting.

Collapsing was my only option. I did manage to turn around and get my ass out of his face before melting into the mattress. Tommy kissed me softly before turning to snuggle his back to my chest and wipe himself down with a handful of tissues. One last little brush of my lips against the tender skin behind his ear, and I tried to catch the curve of his lips, but he turned out the light, and I went with it.

Waking to dim light and movement in my arms, I opened one eye to see Tommy frowning up at what turned out to be a strip of condoms. "Who gets to wear one?" I murmured, hoping he'd unroll one over me.

"Neither of us." He tossed the strip off the edge of the bed. "They expired five months ago."

"I hope you rotate your kitchen stock better than

that." Freshness was for greens and fruits, not for—well, unless it was to use with— *Shut up, Jude. Just because you like him doesn't mean he didn't have a life before you waltzed in.* "How's the lube supply?"

"Plentiful." He waggled the bottle at me. I cupped a palm to catch the squirt of slipperiness. We kissed, carefully, and then I devoted my mouth to his shoulder and my hand to his morning wood. Tommy lay on his back, his cheek against my head, sighing under my ministrations and taking a moment to come back to reality enough to pour more lube into my hand. This I applied to myself, and I turned him to his side.

"Not bare!" He was right to be cautious, but that wasn't what I planned.

"No, not bare." I nestled my erection between his cheeks, wishing I could both thrust along the length of his crack and see myself do it, but I could imagine his ass like the two firm lobes of a peach or a cherry and still reach around to play with his cock. He put his hand back to grab my ass, pulling me to his rhythm while I trailed my tongue along his nape. Less frantic than last night, we thrust together until we had to speed up and then freeze, me a few beats behind him. Tommy's spurts were a throbbing in my palm, and he clenched his buttocks, grabbing me tightly for the last few plunges before I spilled creamy wet heat between our bodies.

Tommy patted my ass, then squeezed, turning once again to lie on his back. "I'll get some fresh wellies for tonight." Those blue eyes made some sideways promises that I wouldn't be around to help him keep.

There was no good way to break this news, and I

hadn't been exactly clear last night. "My plane leaves Heathrow at noon."

The way he folded against the mattress wasn't satiety this time. "I knew this was too good to last. No—" He squeezed my arm when I started to protest. "You didn't make any promises. I'm the one who assumed you'd be in London for a while."

How could I change this? The whirl of thoughts kept me silent. He took it for agreement and tried to get up. "It's all right. I know you've got a life and obligations back in America."

"That isn't it at all!" I scrambled to my knees and found myself talking to his back. "I could get sex anywhere in the world, that isn't—" Wrong thing to say. I knew it the minute it came out of my mouth, and even without that, he'd bolted to the one closable door in the studio. I caught the door full in the face and sacrificed a couple of toes to keeping it from closing. "Ow! Damn it! Give me a minute to think here!"

"Don't worry about the pretty words." His voice was flat, his face expressionless. "You can have first wash." Tommy leaned into the tub to start the water. "It's all right, Jude, you've fucked the fanboy, and now he'll be the perfect one-night stand. No whinging or anything awkward." The sincerity quotient of Tommy's smile was in the negative ranges, and he wouldn't meet my eyes. "I'll even make you a cup of tea before you go."

If I knew what I needed to say, I might have gotten something intelligible out, but I was still standing there, the rushing of the water making more sense than the rushing in my brain when he flipped a towel through the door. "Don't waste the hot water, Jude; I'd like some." He closed the door between us.

I did get in the tub, thinking the water would help me form the right words, but all that happened was that I scrubbed his scent and our fluids off with no plan for getting more on me. My phone shrilled from the pocket of my jeans, lying on the floor where they'd been abandoned in such a hurry last night. Marcie or Sam, no doubt, wanting to know where the hell I was, what the hell I thought I was doing, and telling me to get back to the hotel now, damn it. The phone stopped ringing before I got out of the tub.

Tommy had slid in and left a toothbrush for me, making him less perfect one-night-stand material and more just perfect. Breezing into the bathroom as I came out, he passed me a cup of tea and disappeared behind the shower curtain without a word. If I pulled the curtain aside to talk, assuming I could get the foot out of my mouth or speak around it, he'd probably turn the spray on me. Besides, I didn't deserve another look until I made this right.

"Tommy?" I tried from the doorway.

"Can't hear you over the water!" he called back, and that was my cue to pat my pockets, because anything I left here, I couldn't return for.

He appeared moments later, his face utterly shut off, his words brittle. "I'm off to the market, Jude. Have a nice flight." He locked the door behind us, and without lifting his face for a kiss or any other clue that we might have been intimate in any way, Tommy gave me that "So long, *amigo*" tip of the head and was gone.

The stairs were steeper coming down. Maybe it was me walking with one foot so far in my mouth it was kicking tonsils.

Once on the street, I took a good long look around. It had been dark when I'd arrived, and only the lights and motion inside had lured me into the pub. Now I checked the sign, to see where I'd been. "The Good Man" stood in gold script against a black signboard, but no cheerful bit of folk art or heraldry went with it. No swans, oaks, elephants, castles, harts, gryphons or tradesmen, as might have swung before any other pub, just "The Good Man." And he was. And I'd hurt him. If anyone painted me a pub sign, it would have had an ass on it.

The hotel was only a few blocks over, and when I let myself in, it was to see Sam and Marcie clattering around, packing.

"For someone who's been out catting around all night, you certainly have a long face," Sam observed. "Or did you just drink yourself into a stupor and spend the night in the gutter? You look too tidy for that, but still…."

Okay, that had happened once, and I did manage to wake up with everything but my watch. In no mood to hear about other mistakes I'd made, I sat heavily on the edge of the bed that wasn't tumbled, and barely avoided rolling backward into the dip. The flailing spoiled the intended dramatic gesture of putting my head into my hands.

"We had that problem, too," Marcie chirped. "Good

thing you didn't come home. We ended up using your pillows to fill in the sag."

"Great, like I'd want to rest my head on the same thing you'd propped up your ass with and probably—" I stopped, not liking where that was going. "I feel sorry for whoever gets this room tonight."

"Hah!" Marcie whapped me with a towel she'd picked up off the floor.

"And I was not out catting around." But Tommy might not see it that way.

"So when's the wedding?" Sam had to stick his two cents in.

We'd established two continents ago that he was enough bigger, stronger, and heavier than me that only really dirty fighting would let me prevail, and I didn't want to go through all that trouble to slug him once. "Fuck you. I need to stay in one place long enough to even get to 'I love you'."

"Oh, darn." Sam started to warble "Strangers in the Night."

"Shut up." That was in stereo—Marcie didn't like his singing, and I didn't like his song.

"Staying in one place is not an option. We need to catch the train for the airport shortly." Marcie zipped up her suitcase. "Are you going to change or go like that?"

"I'm staying like this." Clean clothes would be nice, but I was wearing the cleanest I had already.

"Then you won't mess up my not-so careful packing. You could have done your own, *if you'd been here.*" I'd heard the nasty edge in her voice before. "You can zip the case yourself."

"I mean, *I'm staying.*" Tommy could direct me to a laundry.

"You can't stay. We have post-production for the episodes we just filmed," Marcie pointed out.

"And we need to storyboard out the next trip." Sam pushed the box of camera equipment forward. "Come on, give me a hand with this."

He's a strong guy, but the camera case was awkward, and the hotel didn't have an elevator. Wheeling the camera case out the door, Sam headed to the stairs. Thumping down two floors—tell me again why I think this is the third floor but it's referred to as the second?—wasn't good for the equipment, so I followed, grabbing the handle on the back for the journey down.

A black cab stopped for Sam's outstretched hand. We loaded the case in the back, and when I turned to go inside, planning to negotiate another night in the room, Marcie blocked the door.

"Load this." She swung a case at me. "You could have been in a world of hurt if your clothes had beaten you to the airport. Why didn't you answer your phone?"

"Because I didn't want to have this discussion while I was having a more important discussion," I snarled and didn't grab the case.

Sam did, shoving it into the trunk and smacking my back from behind, not so much a blow as a reminder. "Talk nice to Marcie and get in the cab. We need to catch the Heathrow Express out of Paddington." He steered me to the rear door and guarded it until Marcie came back out. With three of us and the luggage, it was a tight fit. Marcie had to lean over Sam for shoulder room.

"The Central American trip is a done deal, but after that, we don't have plans." I found enough breath to make a sideways assault on my guardians. "We can do pub food. Good, bad, gastro, you name it. I have a guide, I think, maybe…." Tommy had to know the best places to get any sort of dish, and if he didn't want to be involved, he'd know someone who would. I shouldn't make assumptions about what he'd be willing to do. I wasn't even sure he'd talk to me.

"We can talk about it, sure." Sam gave Marcie a hand out of the cab and gave me the beady eye until I got out, too. "On the train. Give me a hand with the camera case."

The express train to Heathrow wouldn't take more than twenty minutes, and damn Marcie for not booking us on a train that stopped along the way. Unable to simply escape, I renewed my pitch.

"Pub food isn't going to run more than a couple of episodes, Jude," Marcie pointed out.

"That's hardly the only kind of cuisine available." Why did she have to fight me on this? "There's Indian and Pakistani food. We can talk about how it's changed from its roots, and besides, I love Indian food. Or the great restaurants. I have some friends here on the high end of the business." Oops, wrong tack: Sam and Marcie loved putting me in some humiliating position, choking down things to make the home audience wince. Pitching anything that would make me happy from the start wouldn't appeal to them. "Or the chain restaurants. There are a few that are legendary for awfulness even here. That should be suitably horrible. Really, the series will have a huge variety, and you'll have the next best thing to a vacation once we finish the Central American trip. I'll have done all the legwork."

I searched their faces for something sympathetic and didn't find it. "No doubt I'll get food poisoning somewhere along the way, and you can have all sorts of fun with me and that purple crêpe-y toilet paper." No agreement from either of them, though Marcie looked thoughtful, probably gauging the degree of grossness they could sneak into the show. They'd filmed me crawling across a floor in agony once when something cooked in too much dendê oil got the better of me.

"We can make this work for the show, Jude, but it isn't going to happen today. We need to get back to New York." Sam could shoot me down now, but I was going to have the last word, just not here. I shut up until we were in line at the airline counter.

"I'm going to change my ticket," I told them, and shouldn't have.

"Oh, no, you're not," Sam snapped. "You've got a contract."

"Be reasonable, Jude. You need to come back to New York." Marcie pushed between me and the camera box. "Plan ahead, then take a few days and come back." That was Marcie all over. Plan ahead, have the ducks as much in a row as possible. It worked with hotel rooms and guides, but not for this.

"There won't be anything to come back to." We shoved the baggage forward step by slow step, and I dug in my computer bag, making sure I had the converter I'd need to keep my computer running. It was essential for my plans. I didn't, but Sam did. I fished it out of a zipper pocket on his suitcase.

"Sucks to be you, doesn't it?" Sam slapped my hand away from the coveted silver box.

I slapped back and dared him to take it away—the bared teeth should have been a hint. "I need to charge up before we take off, asshole." The pungent language drew us some looks from others in line.

I did my best to look sad but compliant right up until we reached the head of the line at the ticket counter. A spot at the counter opened up. I let Sam and Marcie go in front of me, and I waited. The next agent, blessedly on the other end of the counter, motioned me over. I scurried, wanting this to be a done deal before my keepers, er, my production crew, noticed the perfidy.

"I'm terribly sorry, but I need to rebook this for the seventeenth of next month." Offering my printed ticket, my passport, and a credit card, I smiled my most winsomely and was rewarded with much tapping of keys and a new itinerary. I left the counter with my baggage and hope, only to run smack into Monster and Sadist.

"Why do you still have your suitcase?" Marcie demanded.

"I might need a change of clothing in the next month?" I hazarded. "The ones I'm wearing could get pretty ripe otherwise."

"You changed your ticket, didn't you?" Captain Obvious shrieked. "You have post-production in New York!"

"*You* have post-production. *I* have voice-over, which is about six hours at most." I'd thought about who did what, and this would work. "If you don't have enough of my babbling on tape already to piece together anything we need, I'll do it over the phone."

"This is a pretty one-sided thing to do to the team, Jude." Sam would side with Marcie in this.

"You don't have any room to talk, friend." I moved us out of the flow of travelers on their way to security. "Did I ever mention to the top brass that you went on that two-day bender in Sydney?" He and Marcie hadn't been getting along so well, and he thought drunk surfing was a fine way to prove his manhood, thus stranding the team and putting us behind schedule while we found new local hosts for two segments. "Your lords and masters still don't know about that, but they would not approve. And even after that dumb-ass stunt and all the scrambling, I *still* didn't make you eat the witchetty grubs with me."

A year later, I could admit they tasted okay if one didn't think about exactly what they were. Sam had to use the tripod to film, between his residual hangover shakes and the dry heaves that started when our host brought out the plate. His gorge rose visibly now.

I was merciless. "They serve crickets with guacamole in Oaxaca, Sam. Aren't we going to be in the vicinity?"

"No. Absolutely not." His color fast approached that of my soup last night.

"'Absolutely not, you aren't going to share my dinner', or 'absolutely not, we stay the hell out of Oaxaca'? If you do the storyboarding without input on every single step from me, you might avoid that. Typing over the Internet and all." I offered him a carrot to go with the stick.

"We'll be in Oaxaca." Marcie's serene smile translated to *Jude will get an extra helping of crickamole for reminding us of that crappy week.*

Actually, I wouldn't. I'd made my mind up a long time ago what to do if we had a repeat of the toasted little snackies with too many legs in Thailand. "Fine, but get it on one take, Marcie, because anything disgusting that requires retakes because you can't get it right, you two get to share."

"Oh, hell no!"

I suddenly feared she was going to puke on me— she'd filmed the witchetty grubs incident reasonably well considering she'd refused to look.

"You're the talent, that's your job."

"Right, and your job is to help me do my job. So, you're going to make it really easy for me to stay in London. No arguments, lots of assistance. I'll be available to you by phone, Internet, and maybe even at hours that approximate daylight on your end. But I'm staying here, because I screwed things up royally this morning, and if I fix it *right now*, I have a chance. If I wait, I don't. And he's—" Remembering Tommy's broken joy and determined nonchalance, I lost my words. "He's worth the effort. And he may not want any part of me now, anyway."

Marcie broke character, meaning she acted human

for the first time since I'd walked through the hotel room door. "You have it bad for this guy, don't you?"

"You could call it that. What I know is that I left him unhappy, and I hate that. We had a really good time—"

"Whoa, big guy, TMI!" Sam interrupted me.

"Shut up, you ass!" Barking at Sam earned me a double glare and a probable extra take of eating something nasty, but I'd had enough. "You two think it's just fine to tell me you fucked on top of my pillows, but you don't want to hear that we *cooked* together. I have never had a better time making eggplant parmesan and my *mother* could have watched us do that!" The rest of his assumptions were probably right, but I didn't care. I was on the attack.

"I have been the third wheel on what amounts to an extended honeymoon for you two, and now when I need to do something for me, that doesn't affect the show, all you can do is give me shit about it!" I probably had enough adrenaline going to take Sam down with one blow, but didn't get to use it.

"You're right, you're right." Both hands up, palms out, Sam backed away. "Relax, Jude, I'll shut up."

Sam wasn't much better than me at being polite— that was as close to an apology as he'd offer, but I understood the code.

"Eggplant parmesan?" Marcie sort of understood the code, but she also understood my cooking tastes. I'd do vegetarian better if it contained some pork.

"His kitchen, his customers, his menu." I didn't relax an inch. "And I am going to go back and see what, if anything, he'll let me help him with tonight."

"And later?"

"I'll be back in New York two days before we leave for Cancun. I'll need a different wardrobe and the brass can see that their star is intact and ready to roll before sending us off. That's the best you're going to get." If Tommy wanted me gone before then, I could probably find something to do besides throw myself in the Thames.

Wearing that faraway look that meant logistics would soon be conquered, Marcie acknowledged that I'd outflanked them. "Okay, then. I'll email you the rough cuts." She hugged me hard. "See you in a month."

"Less if he decides you're an ass." Sam flapped my worst fear at me. "Good luck. See you." One sideways fist whacked his version of goodbye on my shoulder. "Hope it works out, Jude."

"Because I film better when I'm happy?" I didn't trust the good wishes after all the grief.

"You do, but"—he divided his smile between me and Marcie—"you deserve to be happy."

"Thanks." I watched them march off to security, headed back to the train station, and turned my thoughts to Tommy.

Being on the "un" side of "couth" means I have to monitor myself pretty hard when it matters, or any damned thing's likely to come out of my mouth. That's fine when the cameras are rolling and first reactions make best footage, but that's how I'd screwed myself over that morning. Part saying the first thing, and part trying to say the right thing. Nothing went well, and

Tommy got hit with all of my worst gaffes. If I was going to straighten things out with him, I'd have to plan.

Tommy would be back from the market and needed to prep for lunch and dinner service, so at least I knew where I'd find him. Whether it was a good idea to approach an upset man with a cleaver in his hand was another matter.

I'd do some prep work of my own. After sorting out the language, the cabbie who collected me at Paddington figured out I needed a "chemist's shop" and not a "drugstore," and dropped me a block away from The Good Man. I stood in front of a shelf of condoms. What had Tommy called them? Wellies? Weren't those boots? Made of—oh, of course.

If I were to be so fortunate as to use this purchase, I needed something better to say than all the lame-ass things that had been bubbling through my mind. "I'm sorry" might be good in there somewhere, once I could identify what I'd actually done wrong beyond expressing myself clumsily, but hey, couldn't hurt. My suitcase's wheels bumped over the threshold of The Good Man.

It was on the early side for lunch, but a good number of people already took up tables. Tommy might use them as an excuse not to talk yet. Fishing out a pen and my first ticket printout with its big red "Cancelled" stamped over the black printed flight times let me scrawl on the back. "I made some changes. Please talk to me."

Imogen's expression, when she came to take my order, did not bode well for me. "Should I warn you about today's garnishes?" Had her glare been a knife, I'd be fine dice.

"No. Imogen, please, just hand him this." Any soup she served was likely to end up in my lap. Her loyalty to Tommy said a lot for him, and her anger about his state of mind.

She took my ticket, lips pursed thin. "It's not been going well with him today. Will this make things better or worse?"

"Better, I hope." A smile wasn't happening, not with the roiling in my gut worse than anything caused by something I'd eaten for the show, except maybe the Szechuan hot pot. Pleading eyes would have to do. I'd swallowed my first snappy comment. He wouldn't want to hear that there was an unhappy customer at table five.

"We'll see."

I watched her march back to the kitchen, wishing I dared follow, but I wasn't going to invade Tommy's sanctum unasked. If he didn't ask, I might be reduced to lying in wait all day, downing the periodic pint as rent for the space until he closed the kitchen. I crossed my fingers against that possibility. If I couldn't make any kind of case sober, I certainly wouldn't manage shit-faced.

Imogen returned without the active hostility. "You can bring your duffel to the storeroom if you want." I followed her with my cases, hoping this meant I'd be around a while, and at last, I was alone in the heat with Tommy.

He turned the ticket over, looking at front and back, then at me. "Why?"

"Because—" *Because I love the way you smell, I want to*

feel every inch of you, I want to be in the kitchen with someone who loves food as much as you do, because I want about a hundred things, all with you. "Because I want to find out about our possibilities together." I didn't take the last few steps to him, still not sure if I was welcome to come closer. "The flight wasn't my way of making a fast exit."

"It did sound like an excuse to leave." Tommy stopped to check the sizzling contents of a pan. "I was trying to make it easy for you."

"That's just it—I don't *want* to go!" Spinning him around, I forced him to face me, my hands on his upper arms. "I didn't want to go this morning, but you shut down on me so fast."

"Why not? I'm just a lay in London." Tommy's voice was flat, his face expressionless. "You must have turned your back on the blokes in Bangkok and Adelaide without a second thought."

I had, but that was different. "You are *not* just a lay. You're—" Trying to think before I spoke this time, I paused but didn't let him go. "You're Tommy, you're wonderful, you're a chance for me to matter, to make a difference, to—" This took a deep breath to get out. "You're someone who sees me as more than the foodie jerk who'll eat anything for a rating. I was me again last night, don't you see? I was Jude the chef for myself, and I was Jude the man—for you."

"You don't know me." His arms stayed tense under my hands.

"How will that change if I go?" Tommy's own argument was the best one I could make.

And, oh Lord, it was the right one. His smile spread up from his mouth and down from his eyes, and then he was in my arms, his mouth to mine. I would have been content to stay like that until every pan on the stove belched black smoke. Tommy had just that much more awareness of his cooking, though, and broke away enough to use his right hand to shift things around with a spoon. He didn't let go of me. Taking his cue, I became his left hand, and together we were enough of one chef to get one meal plated. Imogen rolled her eyes at the two of us cuddling tight with one arm each and cooking with the other, bringing us back to reality enough to let go.

"What are your plans? Have you thought past changing your flight?" Tommy set up the other two plates using both his own hands, the better to get his waitress out of the way.

Of course, I'd thought of nothing else, but wasn't making assumptions. "Depends on whether or not my companion from last night lets me stay. There's a hotel with saggy mattresses that might have a room, if not."

"I think we can spare your back. At least for tonight." He took a quick look at the slips Imogen had left behind, and they couldn't be the cause for the smile. "Unless you snore."

"Only if I drink too much."

"We'll keep you out of the cellar then." He dished up two fragrant servings of shepherd's pie and started two pans heating. "What else? I can't take time off to go gadding about with you."

"I didn't expect that." Stroking up and down his

back while he worked, I explained my method of escaping my crew. "I made them all sorts of promises about doing research for upcoming shows to keep them from dragging me back to New York in spite of myself." I needed to get this next part out in the open right away. One horrible situation per day was enough. "You can be as much or as little of the show as you want. It's not a condition of me being here for anyone but me." Tommy's sudden dreaminess was a hint of what he'd choose, but I wouldn't push. "And you don't have to decide right away, but I'll need your advice at the very least."

"Imagine that." He leaned down to the oven with basting spoon in hand. "Me advising you on anything."

"Just don't advise me to eat calf's brains," I had to beg. "I can't deal with the texture."

"That's your only quibble with them?" He smiled at me over his shoulder and caught me admiring his ass. "You're in for jellied eel, though."

It couldn't possibly be worse than my Australian bush food adventure. "Just pick the best place for it."

"Only the best." Upright again, Tommy leaned his shoulder against my chest, his face up for a kiss I was only too glad to give him. "I'd give you my very best now, but...."

"But you have this lunch rush going. I understand. Can I help?" Not waiting for the answer, I stuck my hands under the tap.

He handed me an apron, better than any "yes." "We must have some tourists out there. Someone wants a chef's salad."

"I'll do it." Salads are low on the kitchen totem pole; I'd respect Tommy's allowing me in again. "The greens are in the walk-in?"

For the next hour and a half we danced a culinary ballet, twirling around each other while I studied his dishes, making mental notes of where he kept things and what might make his life easier. We'd touched on a few last night, but there were others. And I kept the dish pit clear, though once I'd turned the water off, my stomach rumbled undisguised.

"Bring your luggage." Tommy dished up a large helping of shepherd's pie, and motioned me upstairs. Didn't have to tell me twice; that cup of tea was the only thing I'd had since last night's pea soup.

He pulled off his jacket to reveal a thin white T-shirt, which he'd probably call something else entirely, and snuggled me into his side on the battered brown loveseat under the window, holding the bowl for me so I could inhale the fragrant ground meat and potato. A fine breakfast, punctuated with kisses. Tommy didn't try to talk while I ate, and I didn't provide any commentary beyond noises that sounded a lot like last night's, and a contented sigh when I finished the last drops of broth sopped up with a spoonful of potato.

Turning against him, I draped my arm over Tommy's stomach, prepared to stay as long as he'd let me. How long had it been since someone had fed me just because I was hungry, held me just because it was cozy, or been silent just because it was companionable? Too damned long—and now I was ready to bolt because I'd let my guard down. I told my natural suspicion to back off until we actually heard him whistling the theme from *Sweeney Todd.*

He jerked his arms away at my first stiffening, not holding me down in any way, and then only slowly settled them against me again when I willed myself to calmness. "You don't trust people easily, do you, Jude?"

"No" was too hard to say. I shook my head, my cheek rubbing against the kitchen-scented cotton.

"Why me?" Now Tommy asked my question. It deserved an answer.

"Everyone wants something from me, or they're of some use to me. Or both. And then—" I sat up to look him in the eyes, blue and unnervingly calm, considering that I'd messed with his mind so badly. "Then I found a man who wanted nothing but the pleasure of my company, doing the things I love best, and everything else is a happy bonus. So of course I invited myself into your life. You can run screaming now."

"I'll give it another couple of days." Tommy took a moment to ponder, his mouth quirked to one side. "The things you love best being sex and food?"

"Being food done well and sex done joyfully," I corrected him. I was a very simple soul, but still, were those bad priorities? "And that really was luscious shepherd's pie."

"Well, that's one down. Why don't we see about the joyful sex?" Putting his arms out to me, he let me melt back against him, grateful as hell that he'd seen through me. "I haven't been out to buy condoms. It didn't seem like there was much point."

No, not after I'd left. "In a fit of extreme hopeful-ness, I got some."

"Seeing to my *mise en place* again, are you?" Tommy's smile was broad enough to reveal the twisted bicuspid that didn't quite hide behind the canine, and I wondered how many other ways I could bring that grin. Right now I covered it with my own lips, and we quit talking.

Lord, Tommy was as oral as I, his tongue finding mine for soft strokes that grew firmer, wilder, sliding across my cheek and down my neck. Taking time to really explore would have to wait. Right then I needed more than anything to feel the strength of his desire, to know his urgency, to be welcomed in all at once. We tried to strip each other and succeeded in landing on the floor in a tangle of denim and jersey that only came off when we remembered to kick away our shoes.

He splayed me across the giant cabbage roses on the floor, the worn Axminster carpet scraping my butt while he kissed his way across my belly, rubbed his face across the skin, and brought me curving up to implore him not to stop with the one little lick across the head of my erection. He only laughed.

Strong, scarred hands pinned my hips, and he set to slurping me in, sucking me down with abandon. Twining my fingers into his hair, I could only wish to reach more of him. He made me wait, until suddenly I couldn't wait any longer, exploding from somewhere deep within.

He held me in his mouth until the shaking stopped, then brought a few more shudders in the long, warm letting go. "Turn about," I wheezed, meaning fair play, but he swiveled, bringing his haunch into patting range. "Sit on the couch."

I could get to my knees unaided, but didn't try to rise farther. Tommy bent to me, lips to lips for a moment, the tang of my fluids on his tongue. A moment to rest against his chest, to hear his heart thudding, and then my mouth was against his cock, which had been a hard and pulsing column against my chest while I listened to the warm beat of his life. I savored him, engulfing, feeling the play of textures, soft, hard, velvet and scratch, licking the salt and breathing the musk, until he too was undone, filling my mouth.

Tommy's heart beat hard, the wild pounding calming under my ear when I slipped my arms around him to lean against his chest again. The soft hairs tickled the side of my nose, his strong arms across my shoulders reminding me that I had come much too close to flying away from this joy.

"I'm glad you came back," Tommy eventually murmured into my hair, where his lips had been resting. "And I'd love to stay like this the rest of the afternoon, but I still haven't decided on what goes with the chops for the special."

"Mmmm, what was nice at the market this morning?" I could think like a chef with the part of my brain that wasn't focused on skin pressed to skin. A small part, true.

"Cherry tomatoes, fennel to braise with orange, some Kalamata olives to broil in bacon for starters. Granny Smith apples. I thought I'd do a *tarte tatin* with those. I only do one sweet, take it or leave it." His little sigh reminded me he'd said he wasn't much of a pastry chef.

Even so, a one-man operation had only so much time. The *patissieres* often came to work in the early morning and were done with their magic before lunch service started in the finer restaurants. Their relatively good hours earned them the reputation as the wusses of the culinary world, but how many people with conflicting needs for oven space could one kitchen accommodate? When some of my old line cooks got to slamming around, every cake in the place would fall flat. Hell, I'd slain a cake or two with my temper.

"It wasn't a terribly balanced selection," Tommy concluded.

"But not undoable." I'd unbalanced him; I needed to help him recover. "What do you have on hand in the way of cheese?" My baguette last night had Camembert inside it, which had been trendy thirty years ago but was uncontroversial now.

"Some feta, quite a bit of Boursin. Small amounts of three or four others, salad quantities, really."

"Then"—I paused to kiss his breastbone—"we use the tomatoes, the Boursin, and a few of the olives for a savory *tarte tatin*, very pretty next to a chop, braise the fennel as you planned, and if I may have a couple of liters of stout, we'll make apple-Guinness crumbles. Two kinds of *tarte tatin* will confuse the diners. You do have a lot of boats?"

"I'm not sure what I have is what you're asking for. We'd best check. But—" Tommy did a concerned double-take when my knees creaked on my way to upright. Blame twenty-plus years on concrete flooring. "But since I screwed up my purchases, I shouldn't depend on you to extricate me."

I extricated him from the loveseat, taking the opportunity to pull him close once he was on his feet. "I'm here, I'm willing. Put me to work."

"You're here now." Tommy held me and didn't complete the thought aloud.

"Yeah, I have an expiration date. I'm on tour again the middle of next month for around three weeks. Not negotiable—I *have* to be there. Then planning and filming for the eels and whatever else, so I'll at least be in the vicinity if you're still talking to me, and we decide from there." I had to warn him. "Tommy, I am an irritating cuss. You might be glad to get rid of me."

His arms went tight around me. "Then again, I might not."

BREAKING THE FAST

The calendar had tormented Tommy for the last three weeks, ever since Jude had flown out of Heathrow to São Paulo. Phone calls were no substitute for the warmth of his lover in their bed or the skill of his hands in the kitchen—Jude had probably forgotten more about food than Tommy would ever know.

To hear the huskiness in Jude's voice from the other side of the Atlantic describing the joys of a breakfast of *bolinhos* and *pastels* doused in hot sauce made Tommy want that desire for himself. He'd never be the fiery peppers in anyone's meal; no, he was just plain old Tommy Bell, landlord of the Good Man, and would-be chef. He wasn't in Jude's league, and every time Jude flew away to film another set of episodes for his show, Tommy worried that he'd find someone more exciting in a far-flung place and wouldn't be flying back.

But those calls, just about every day, said yes, yes, Jude would return. Tommy hadn't been best pleased when Jude tried instigating phone sex with his voice slurred from one too many *caipirinhas,* but he'd gone along with it, desperate to feel connected. Other nights, when Jude's voice was clear but his belly overstuffed with *moquecas* or grilled piranha, they didn't try for arousal, but talked about things that mattered. Best of all, there had been calls when Jude hadn't overindulged in anything on behalf of his show. Then they'd talked, and then their voices dropped; they'd made love to one another with words and their own hands across the thousands of miles of Atlantic.

Jude's nights in Brazil kept Tommy awake into the wee hours, but he didn't begrudge the lost sleep. There'd be no call tonight—Jude had caught the red-eye express from São Paulo.

Tommy didn't want to leave his little flat above the pub. He'd have to go downstairs eventually to prep for lunch, but Jude's plane had landed in Heathrow while Tommy was at the market. Jude had to find his luggage, get through Immigration, and catch the Express to Paddington. He couldn't possibly get here for at least another twenty minutes. He'd be tired, rumpled, and hungry after the long flight. He'd need breakfast.

The whole world fed Jude with things weird and wonderful; what could Tommy give him? Would beans on toast be one more unfamiliar thing to choke down, one more meal that said, "You are a stranger here"? Tommy checked the pantry in his little kitchen, where breakfast was the only meal he ate. Weetabix, no, not special, and his hand didn't even pause on the tin of coffee; he'd not push Jude to stay awake after eight hours of sitting bolt-upright in a flying pilchard tin.

He settled on shirred eggs, throwing the little ramekins of egg and butter into the *bain marie,* closing the door on the oven to let the egg set up. That should be familiar enough, shouldn't it?

Jude would have other hungers, too, but would he be too tired? No matter, Tommy would be happy to do nothing more than dip the bread soldiers into the runny yolk and hold them to Jude's lips, perhaps seasoning them with a kiss.

Jude might have slept on the plane. He'd still be tired from traveling but... Tommy checked the clock, thinking of traffic from Paddington to the pub. Not long... He stripped and replaced the apron, hoping. Footsteps sounded on the stairs—Tommy posed against the table to study a cookbook chucked open upside down. Jude's key turned in the lock, the squeak announcing the door swinging open.

Lifting his eyes from the unreadable words, Tommy watched the smile spread across Jude's face. He couldn't hold the tableau one moment longer—dashing across the tiny sitting room, he flung himself into Jude's arms, clutching, pressing, opening his mouth to the onslaught of Jude's tongue.

The first desperate kiss broken, Tommy buried his face into Jude's neck, inhaling faint traces of tropics and the tang of the journey on his lover, whose hands lay hot against Tommy's back. Jude's cheek rubbed hard against Tommy's head, and his ribcage expanded past a normal breath—that should fill him with the scent of Tommy and baking eggs, with the scent of welcome.

"Oh, Tommy." Jude held him more tightly, swaying slightly; Tommy could feel him pressing lips against skin. "It's good to be home."

JUDE AND TOMMY'S
GUINNESS-APPLE CRUMBLE

Ingredients

   440ml (1 12 ounce can) Guinness

   180g (3/4 cup +2Tbsp) brown sugar

   1 Tbsp soft butter

   salt

   9 tart cooking apples, peeled, cored and sliced

For the crumble topping

   65g (1/3 cup) sugar

   45g (1/3 cup) all purpose flour

   3 Tbsp rolled oats

   3 Tbsp butter

   salt

   100g (1/2 cup) grated Dubliner cheese or sharp
cheddar (optional)

For the Caramel

Guinness cooking liquid (pour out of the baked crumble)

2 Tbsp butter

To assemble:

Preheat oven to 180C/350F; butter a baking dish.

Whisk together Guinness, sugar and a pinch of salt. Set aside.

Put apple slices into the baking dish and pour the Guinness mixture over. Dot the top of the apples with little pats of butter.

For the crumble:

Rub together the sugar, flour, oats, butter and a pinch of salt. Scatter over the apples and top with cheese. Bake for 60 minutes or until the cheese melts and the top is golden. Remove from the oven.

For the Caramel

Spoon off as much of the cooking liquid as possible into a saucepan. Over medium high heat reduce the liquid by half, stirring occasionally. Stir butter into the thickened liquid. Let cool slightly before serving. Note: if you skip the cheese, the cooking liquid reduces more and you may not have enough for this step. It's yummy anyway.

Jude and Tommy make this in individual oven-proof dishes dishes and reserve part of the Guinness at the beginning for the caramel. Reduce cooking time to 45 minutes for the small dishes.

ABOUT THE AUTHOR

P.D. Singer lives in Colorado with her slightly bemused husband, one proto-adult, and a deficiency of cats. She's a big believer in research, first-hand if possible, so the reader can be quite certain Pam has skied down a mountain face-first, been stepped on by rodeo horses, acquired a potato burn or two, and will never, ever, write a novel that includes sky-diving.

When not writing, playing her fiddle, or skiing, she can be found with a book in hand.

Follow the adventures at http://PDSinger.com or drop a note at PD.Singer@RockyRidgeBooks.com.

Keep up with the latest from P.D Singer, and our other Rocky Ridge authors by joining our newsletter.

Find Pam here:

PDSinger.com
PD.Singer@RockyRidgeBooks.com

A TASTE FROM SPOKES:

The big silver sedan blew past close enough to touch, and he damned near did. Christopher Nye shook his fist at the receding vehicle, once he'd wrestled his bike under control.

"Stupid gas-burner!" Stu Fallon made his point with a one-fingered salute. "There's a whole other lane they could have used—why'd they have to nearly run us down?"

"Most people around Boulder give bikes enough room." Christopher shot a wary glance behind lest some other three thousand pound weapon guided by a moron was sneaking up on him. "There's enough cyclists on the road, you'd think they'd all understand."

"I'd like them to get sucked into a slipstream and then ask if they had enough room," Stu grumbled, but he'd already gotten to speed again, and Christopher wouldn't waste the breath to help him complain. At least this bright, crisp January day didn't have the additional hazard of snow, which made it perfect for a brisk run out to the wide spot on the road that was Hygiene, Colorado. Still a couple of puddles at the side of the road though.

Bright jerseys and spandex leggings dotted the roads in and around Boulder. Fewer than in June, a rainbow of cyclists hugged the roads' shoulders, even in winter. Christopher and Stu would have less traffic to worry about once they reached the north edge of town. Then they wouldn't be run off the road every mile or so.

Close to thirty miles of gentle rolls and near flat called to him. Christopher had just tightened his chain and adjusted the derailleurs, his leggings were comfortably worn in and the chamois lining greased heavily; nothing on man or bike would chafe. He had layers he could peel down if the breeze dropped, but the mid-fifties temps probably wouldn't persuade him to remove the arm warmers he'd put on with a short-sleeved jersey. With a last tweak to his helmet and sunglasses, Christopher followed Stu up the road.

"Checking out my butt again?" Stu called, once they made the turn onto Jay Road.

"It isn't any more attractive than it was last time. How you can ride so many miles and still have such a scrawny ass is beyond me." Christopher sped up and around Stu, who dropped back to trail in Christopher's wake. They'd take turns fighting the air, letting the other draft. It wasn't the same degree of relief as riding in the midst of a peloton would be, but even one rider to create a slipstream made a huge difference in how hard they had to work.

Christopher didn't like thinking about the peloton, that massed group of cyclists riding only inches apart. His last race had gone smash when he'd been hemmed in on all sides. Someone had thrown an elbow at a rider in front, sending a ripple of motion sideways until someone hadn't reacted fast enough or accurately enough. Wheel caught wheel then, handlebars caught hips, and twenty cyclists had gone down in a tangle of metal and rubber. Christopher had gotten off lightly for meeting the road and someone else's bike, leaving some skin on the pavement and taking a cleat mark on his chest, but he'd shied from riding with a lot of people since. The pros and the group I/II riders could probably have stayed upright and possibly even disciplined the elbow-thrower, but the group IV riders like Christopher didn't have those skills yet. And if he couldn't make himself get back into the peloton, he never would.

But the season was young—he didn't have to apply for his racing license again for another month or two. Training was enough, even with the inadequate scenery perched on Stu's saddle. He had zero interest in that particular ass anyway. Stu was a friend, straight, and the best matched riding partner Christopher had. Thinking boner-inducing thoughts while trying to maintain tempo for two hours was only going to interfere with getting fit after a month of holiday indulgence and weather-enforced idleness.

They'd swapped off the lead again after they'd reached the true country roads, letting Christopher look around more than at the road ahead. Enough breeze came off the hills to their west that he and Stu both zipped their jackets to the throat. Cottonwoods along the creek beds made brown lace against the fiercely blue sky, and last year's grasses at the side of the road whispered drily at their passage. He felt good, swinging along at seventy rpm in a gear that wasn't his tallest, but that would be for later in the season. For now, maintaining his pace without challenging his anaerobic threshold was the goal. That and enjoying himself.

The road grew narrower, the Ute Highway being on the same scrawny side as Stu's behind, but the reservoir to their right sparkled in the sun. One pickup truck had gone around them since they'd made the last turn.

"Coming up on the left!"

The yell was upon them almost as soon as the riders were—a pack of fast-moving cyclists zipped by, a blur of turquoise and black.

"Let's catch them and draft!" Stu's enthusiasm had to be twice his speed, which picked up substantially.

"Fat chance." Christopher accelerated too, even though the other riders were pulling away without looking like they were working for it.

"Are those the Garmin-Sharp guys?"

"Nah, they wear blue with black and white trim." Christopher had cheered the Boulder-based pro team in the *Tour de France* and every other race he'd been able to see.

"Wow." Stu dropped back to their previous pace. "They passed us like nothing and that one guy is sitting up to take his jacket off." The team hadn't stopped, but one of the backs now sported unbroken turquoise instead of a black V.

Wow, indeed. The bike handling and speed that had just blown by on what had to be an easy training ride made Christopher feel like he'd barely graduated from a tricycle. Those riders could have cut their racing teeth as juniors, with decent equipment and some support from their family. Or town, if any of them were Belgian— Belgian riders grew up on bone-rattling cobblestone streets where every passer-by could assess their form. Maybe some of them were from Italy, where small boys dreamed of growing up to be the next Fausto Coppi or Gianni Bugno. Or France, where a three week stage race was practically a national holiday and a stage winner never had to buy his own drinks again. A few might be Americans, but they didn't learn to race on a discount store bike with five unusable gears.

He'd started years too late to dream of belonging to the elite, but he could expect to get from Boulder to Hygiene and back in under an hour and a half. Christopher pulled back into the present, adjusting his grip and his expectations.

Once home, Christopher opened a new document on his laptop, thinking back to the dozen riders who'd sped past him.

Antano-Clark may have just arrived in Boulder, but they're already blowing the locals off the roads. Looking for the advantages of living and training at altitude, this newly formed team hopes to make stars out of such workhorses as Luca Biondi, formerly of

Duclos-Wurth, who finished a surprise sixth in last year's Paris-Nice stage race, and Rolf Knecht, from Kastibank…

He finished the article, built mostly from press releases, some scuttlebutt, and what he'd seen that day. Should he save it for Stu to proofread? Maybe not this time—he could do without the shit Stu would give him on the subject. His editor could find the stray commas for once. Emailing it to *CycloWorld*, Christopher considered that his other great dream, seeing his byline in print, had been a lot more achievable and even built upon his cycling. His parents never chided him about his expensive journalism degree turning into tiny articles and an evil day job in a shop: he'd get there. Maybe he should start carrying the Nikon currently gathering dust on the bookshelf.

Picking out faces to attach to names simply hadn't been possible today. Christopher couldn't know if he'd seen sprinters or climbers, *domestiques* or the general classification stars. The pictures from last May's *CycloWorld* weren't helping him figure it out, but he stopped on a Duclos-Wurth profile article, just to try. Damn but Luca Biondi had a nice ass.

Pro cyclist Luca Biondi lives for the race. For the star of Team Antano-Clark, victory lies within his grasp—if he can outdistance 200 other hopefuls, avoid suspicion from race officials, and keep his lieutenant more friend than foe. Luca also has secrets, and eyes for amateur cyclist and journalist Christopher Nye.

Christopher understands Luca's need to keep their relationship under wraps, but chafes at hiding in the shadows of his lover's career. He's ready to cheer Luca's victories, but he knows too well how triumph can turn to tears. While Christopher's heart sees Luca the man, his inner journalist—and his editor—sees the cycling world's biggest scoop.

From the jagged curves of the Colorado Rockies to the viciously steep Belgian hills, Luca can ride out any bumps—except rumors.

A few words in the wrong ear could crash everything. With miles between them, hints of scandal, and Luca's fierce need to guard his reputation, a journalist might have to let go of the biggest story of his career or risk forcing his lover to abandon the race. Christopher and Luca face a path more treacherous than any road to the summit.

Read the rest of Spokes in MOBI, EPUB and print.